The Blue Lobster

by Robin Taylor-Chiarello

Illustrated by Lisa Bohart

the Peppertree Press

Sarasota, Florida

For information regarding permission,
call 941-922-2662 or contact us at our website:
www.peppertreepublishing.com or write to:
the Peppertree Press, LLC.
Attention: Publisher
1269 First Street, Suite 7
Sarasota, Florida 34236

ISBN: 978-1-936343-84-3

Library of Congress Number: 2011926816

Printed in the U.S.A.

Printed April 2011

For Thomas, my very own blue lobster.

Many thanks to my husband Bob, sons Stephen and Joseph, daughter Amy, daughter-in-law Gina and son-in-law Steve for their love and support...and hugs to my granddaughters Grace and Maddie and special friends Ella and Taxi. May you all enjoy my books, written from the heart.

Love, Robin (Grandy)

I heard them talking when I was trapped today...
I am one in a million or so they say...

It is hard to believe
you're judged by a shell,
the shock of my color
just doesn't sit well.

6

I have been living alone under the sea
no other lobsters will play with me.

Scurrying around the ocean floor,
dealing with every unopened door.

I would knock on their rock, say, "How do you do?
I am Mr. Homarus Americanus and just like you!"

"OK...I am blue, no doubt about that,
come from under that rock
and we can have a nice chat."

We could talk about prey fish,
the burrows we know...
mollusks and plant life and places we go.

"I am distinctive and different
I must grant you that!"
Maybe they would like me if I sported a hat...

14

If not a bright hat,
maybe wild pants!

"If that doesn't work I'll show them my dance..."

"Oh!, I can curl my tail
to swim backwards you know,
it's a basic life skill
and not just for show!"

But no one would befriend me,
I was lonely, in fact.

When I wandered alone
into a oneway trap.

So now I am here at the "Kettle of Fish"
hoping not to become tonight's special dish!

People walk by... they comment I'm blue...
Cooked red lobsters is all that they knew.

The owners appear with a shiny new tank...
Spotlights, a sign- "No this is not a prank!"

No this is Not a Prank.
Come See!
Mr. Homarus Americanus

"I am one in a million or so they say,
I'm the celebrity lobster and here to stay."

So be kind to things that are different than you,
for they may become a celebrity too!

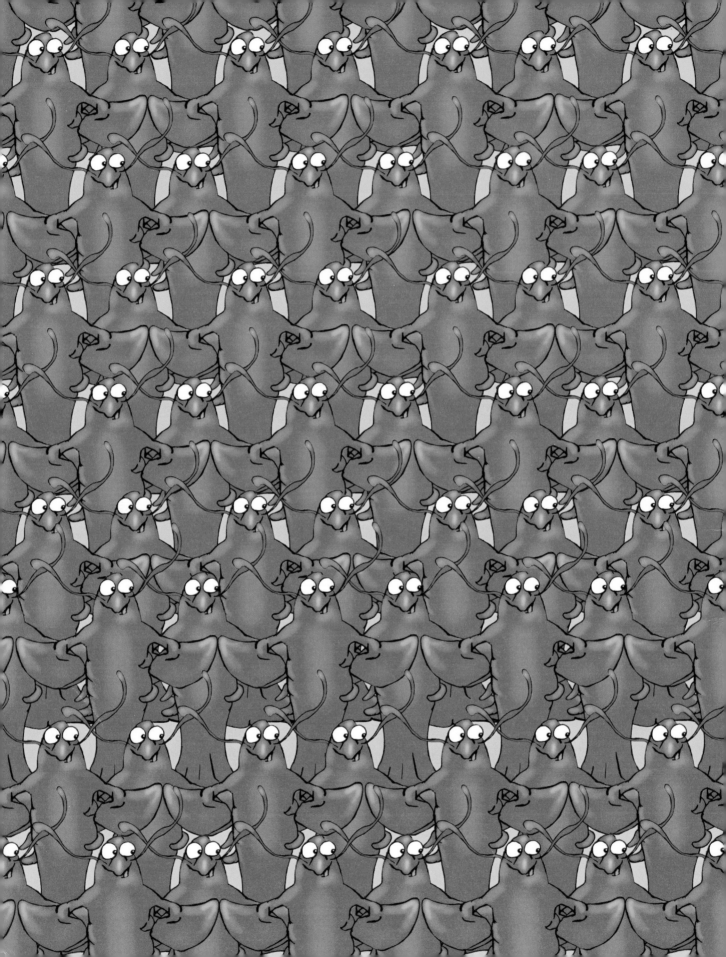

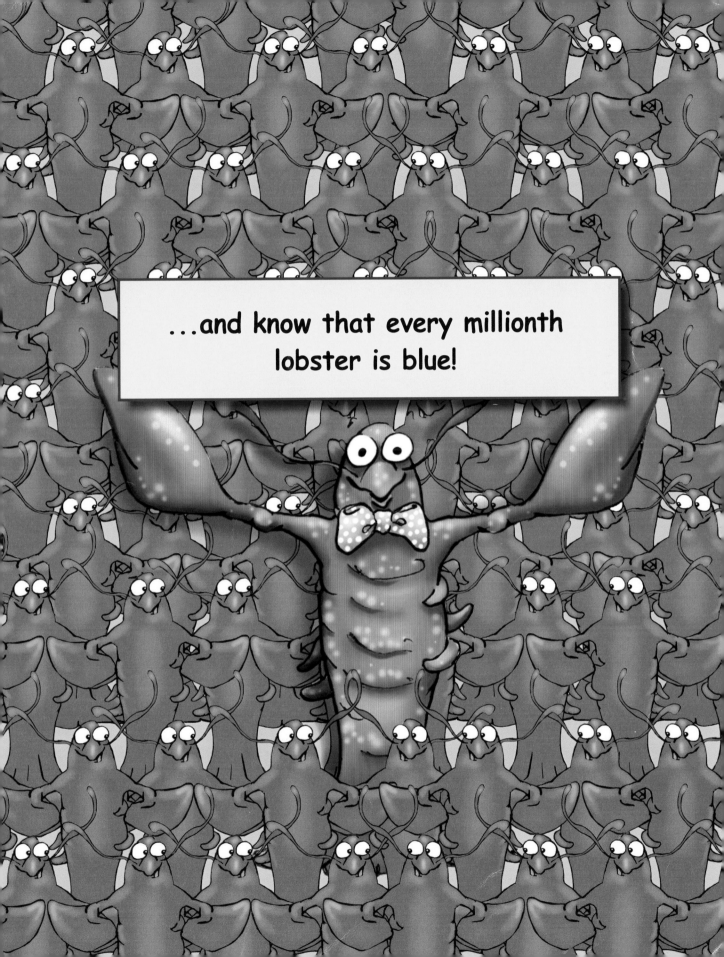

CPSIA information can be obtained
at www.ICGtesting.com
Printed in the USA
LVXC01n0928191017
552987LV00001B/1